DiNKiN DiNGS
AND THE CURSE OF
CLAWFINGERS

To Ruby, who makes everything less scary ~ GB

To Honor, Grace and Arthur –
Kent's foremost Dinkinites ~ PW

Also available:

Check out Dinkin's Bebo page at:
www.bebo.com/dinkindings

And visit Guy Bass at:
www.guybass.com

STRIPES PUBLISHING
An imprint of Magi Publications
1 The Coda Centre, 189 Munster Road,
London SW6 6AW

A paperback original
First published in Great Britain in 2009

Text copyright © Guy Bass, 2009
Illustrations copyright © Pete Williamson, 2009

ISBN: 978-1-84715-105-6

Printed and bound in the UK.
10 9 8 7 6 5 4 3 2

DINKIN DINGS
AND THE CURSE OF CLAWFINGERS

GUY BASS

Illustrated by PETE WILLIAMSON

Stripes

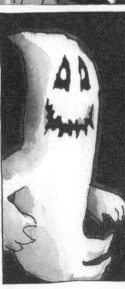

THE (TERRIFYING) TRUTH ABOUT DINKIN DINGS

Dinkin Dings was afraid of everything. And not just actual scary things like diving into a swimming pool full of alligators or having a tea party in the middle of a busy motorway. No, he was afraid of pretty much completely and utterly *everything*. Apart from, that is:

1. The monster under his bed
2. The skeleton in his cupboard
3. The ghost outside his window

In fact, they were his best friends.

He called them the *Frightening Things*.

TOPPER THAN THE TOPPEST TOP SECRET

Homework: 48% complete
Room tidying: 22% complete
Ultimate invention: 79% complete

"Dinkin! Have you seen my hairdryer?" called Dinkin's mother. It was 18:18 on an unseasonably cold Thursday the eighteenth of May.

"Umm ... no," shouted Dinkin from his bedroom. He looked down at the hairdryer, lying in pieces on the desk in his bedroom, along with a large assortment of other objects. As he heard his mum's footsteps coming up the stairs, he quickly grabbed the Complete Concealment Cover-Up Cover™ (an old sheet with the words "NOTHING

TO SEE HERE" written on it) and threw it over them.

"What are you up to, Dinkin Dings?" asked Dinkin's mother, as she burst into the room. She spotted the sheet and narrowed her eyes suspiciously. "What's under that sheet?"

"Nothing," said Dinkin, nervously. "There's nothing to see here."

"That had better not be another one of your inventions – we're still clearing up the mess from the last one," said his mother. Actually, Dinkin's last invention wasn't all *that* messy – it had only destroyed Dinkin's chest of drawers, which may or may not have been haunted. *Much* worse were, for example:

THE ANTI-ANT MACHINE
(24% Ant Infestation)

THE ANTI-ANTELOPE MACHINE
(43% Zoo Closure)

THE ANTI-ANSWERING MACHINE
MACHINE (61% Air Pollution)

THE ANTI-AUNTIE MACHINE
(100% Auntie Evacuation)

"It's top secret," explained Dinkin. "Topper than the toppest top secret. It's really safer if you don't know."

"I'm not even going to ask," sighed his mother. "But I want that hairdryer back on my dressing table in the next two minutes.

And please, whatever you're doing, try not to break anything."

As his mother made her way downstairs, Dinkin pulled back the Complete Concealment Cover-Up Cover™ and stared at the dismantled hairdryer. He took what he didn't need and tried his best to tape the rest back together.

"That'll have to do," said Dinkin to himself. He couldn't waste any more time, not with so much important work to do – he was only hours away from completing his *ultimate invention* – a device of such power, such indescribable indescribableness that it was almost totally impossible to describe. But one thing was certain – once his ultimate invention was complete, he would never have to be scared of anything ever again.

Dinkin took a piece of paper out of his pocket and unfolded it. On it was a long list of seemingly everyday objects. He put a tick next to the word HAIRDRYER. There were only four items left unticked.

TOILET ROLL TUBE
TV REMOTE CONTROL
BATTERIES (AA)
OLD TELEPHONE

Dinkin made his way downstairs into the sitting room. He found the remote control and slipped it into his pocket.

"Evening, Dink!" said his father loudly, as he strode into the room.

" **AAAH!** "

screamed Dinkin, running for cover behind the coffee table. His father had a terrible habit of appearing suddenly and being "accidentally" terrifying.

"Didn't mean to startle you, old chap," continued Dinkin's dad, as he looked for the remote control. "Fancy watching the cricket with me?"

"No, thanks," said Dinkin, shuddering. Dinkin found all sport thoroughly petrifying, but cricket was so boring that he was terrified of blacking out from watching just a few seconds. It came second only to golf as the most terrifyingly unwatchable thing on TV.

One down, three to go.

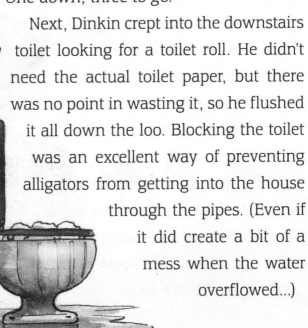

Next, Dinkin crept into the downstairs toilet looking for a toilet roll. He didn't need the actual toilet paper, but there was no point in wasting it, so he flushed it all down the loo. Blocking the toilet was an excellent way of preventing alligators from getting into the house through the pipes. (Even if it did create a bit of a mess when the water overflowed...)

He put the toilet roll tube into his pocket, and as the water began to bubble over the top of the loo, he made his way into the kitchen.

Two down, two to go.

In the kitchen, Dinkin nervously pulled open the deeply frightening *Drawer of Random Stuff That Doesn't Quite Belong Anywhere Else*. He donned his De-Randomizing Gloves™ (an old pair of mittens and some packing tape to prevent any randomness from leaking in) and rummaged around for some batteries. After sifting through some elastic bands and a box of keys that may or may not unlock something otherworldly (like the door to the Dimension of a Million Doors) he finally spotted a packet of batteries. He retrieved two (more than enough to power his ultimate invention) and made his way back upstairs.

Three down, one to go.

Dinkin sat down at his desk and laid the objects out. He was only hours away from never being afraid again, but getting the last thing on his list was going to be terrifyingly tricky. He knew where the old telephone was, because he remembered his dad saying that even though it was ancient and outdated, he couldn't bring himself to throw it away. It had gone where all ancient, outdated things went (apart from Grandma Dings, who went to the alarmingly creepy Slightview Retirement Village). If Dinkin was going to complete his ultimate invention, he would need to venture to a place he had never dared to go before, a place so terrifying that it made the middle of a volcano seem like a good place for an afternoon nap.

But he wasn't going there alone.

This was a job for the Frightening Things!

WHERE FRIGHTENING THINGS FEAR TO TREAD

Slippers eaten: 1
Burps burped: 1
Ultimate inventions started
(but not finished): 5

Dinkin waited for the midnight hour. Soon, his three best friends would be at his side, ready, willing and able to help him in this, his hour of need (or at least, he'd be able to hide behind them when things got *really* scary). Dinkin took the Ancient Summoning Parchment from under the Ancient Summoning Mattress and assumed the Ancient Summoning Position. After a quick sip of Ancient Summoning Water (which happened to be exactly the same as tap water) he began the Ancient Summoning Chant:

"Frightening Things, Frightening Things,
Creep from the gloom,
Crawl from the shadows and into my room,
Frightening Things, Frightening Things,
Come to my aid,
Save me from danger (and being afraid!)"

The cupboard door and window burst open! Edgar the skeleton emerged from the cupboard, checking nervously to see if he still had all his limbs, while Arthur the ghost flew through the window and began flitting anxiously from one corner of the room to the other.

"What is it? What happened? Is it the end of the world again? It's the end of the world, isn't it? I knew it! I had a funny feeling in my ectoplasm! Duck and cover!" squealed Arthur, flying through Dinkin's desk and hiding underneath.

"Oh do shut up, Arthur, I'm sure it's not the end of the world," said Edgar, examining his elbows for looseness. "I mean it's not as if the end of the world is just going to happen without warning, is it? Wait ... *is it*? Has the unthinkable happened? Oh, Dinkin, don't try and spare our feelings – if the world's ending just come right out and say it. Oh mercy, I can tell by the look on your face! It *is* the end of the world! But there's so much afterlife left to live!"

"It's not the end of the world," said Dinkin, firmly. "But it could be at any moment – danger is everywhere! That's why I'll need all of your help to— Hang on, where's Herbert?"

Dinkin, Edgar and Arthur waited for a moment, expecting the monster to crawl out from under the bed. After a few seconds, a sudden noise broke the silence.

BUUUUUUURRRP!

"Herbert! Stop eating my stuff!" said Dinkin, peering under his bed. There was Herbert, happily tucking into one of Dinkin's slippers. "Oh, great – I just had those disinfected! Twice!"

"Sorry, Dinkin," said Herbert through a mouthful of slipper. "I always get hungry when I'm nervous. And what with the world ending and all..."

"For the last time, the world is not ending! Now come out here – I have something to show you..." said Dinkin, leaping off the bed. He grabbed the Complete Concealment Cover-Up Cover™ and pulled it back to reveal a strange assortment of everyday objects, including:

4 coaster wheels (from Dinkin's dad's favourite armchair)

6 spoons (tea and soup)

7 party poppers (Dinkin had to handle them with extra special care as he was terrified of both things that popped and parties)

1 large lunchbox

1 stapler

3 pencils (blunted to make them less scary)

1 model aeroplane

1 can opener

2 umbrellas (material removed)

1 golf ball

1 roll of sticky tape

1 bottle of superglue

various bits and pieces from Dinkin's mum's hairdryer

...and of course, one toilet roll tube, one TV remote control and two AA batteries.

"What's it all for?" asked Herbert, wondering if he was allowed to eat any of it.

"It's my ultimate invention! Or at least it will be when I've built it. An invention of such indescribable indescribableness that it is almost impossible to—" began Dinkin, but Edgar interrupted.

"Just a minute – another ultimate invention?" said the skeleton. "This isn't going to be like the last ultimate invention, is it? Or the one before that?"

In fact, there had been five previous "ultimate inventions"...

1) The Virtually Indestructible Cybernetic Terror-Obstructor Robot – or V.I.C.T.O.R for short (Ultimate Invention factor: 0.1)

2) The Tension Prevention Engine (Ultimate Invention factor: 2.8)

3) The All-in-one Anti-AAAAAAH! Alarm (Ultimate Invention factor: 3.3)

4) Dinkin's Dedicated Dread Defeating Device (Ultimate Invention factor: 4.7)

5) The Ultimator 5000 (Ultimate Invention factor: 6.1)

...none of which had ever been finished.

That was the trouble with being scared of everything – the minute Dinkin put his mind to a solution for one horrible fear, a new, more terrifying terror emerged! The world was getting scarier by the second, and Dinkin was helpless to do anything about it. That is, until now.

"This ultimate invention is nothing like those other ultimate inventions!" cried Dinkin, his eyes wild. "This is the real thing!"

"I'm fairly sure that's what you said last time, and who knows where that one ended up," said Edgar.

"This is different! This will be ten times as ultimate as any other ultimate invention," said Dinkin. "All it needs is the final piece – the old telephone – and it will be complete! But for that we need to go into ... the LOFT."

"**AAAAAAAHH!** Not the LOFT!" screamed the Frightening Things. They couldn't believe what they were hearing!

"I can't believe what I'm hearing!" said Edgar. "You told us never to go into the loft!"

"You said it was the most terrifying place in the house!" squealed Arthur.

"You said CLAWFINGERS lives there!" said Herbert.

"AAA-AAAA-AH!" screamed the Frightening Things again. "Clawfingers" was the evil, child-hating loft-creature who, according to Dinkin, lived in the loft. All Dinkin "knew" was that he had just one arm, with a hideous, misshapen claw on the end ... and that he liked to use it to chop children into little pieces. Not that Dinkin had ever seen him, of course. In fact, Dinkin had never so much as been near the loft. Even when the hatch in the ceiling was closed, Dinkin would run past it as fast as he could.

And whenever Dinkins dad lowered the ladder and opened the hatch, Dinkin would scamper into his Fortress of Ultimate Protection (which, even with some recent improvements, was still basically some cardboard boxes tied together with string). Even when his father had come back down and promised for the forty-fifth time that there *was* no Clawfingers and the loft was perfectly safe, Dinkin would stay in his fortress for the rest of the day.

"This is a terrible idea," said Edgar, trying to stop his knees from knocking together. "What do we need a phone for anyway?"

"To enter the ultimate invention activation code, or course! Do you think my ultimate invention just has an 'ON' button?" said Dinkin, shaking his head in despair.

"How silly of me..." sighed Edgar. "Well then, how about getting your father to get the telephone? Clawfingers always seems to leave him alone..."

"I can't ask Dad! I promised him I wouldn't invent anything else for a whole *month* after the *Anti-Auntie Machine* thing..." whispered Dinkin. He did feel a bit guilty about his Auntie June ending up in hospital, but then it was 92% likely that she was a vampire, so it was really for the best. "Look, I know it seems  crazy, but once my ultimate invention is finished, we won't have to worry about Clawfingers ever again. We won't have to worry about *anything* ever again!"

"Really? Not ever?" said Arthur.

"Not ever ever?" added Herbert.

"Not ever ever *ever*!" replied Dinkin, impatiently. "Now are you with me, or not?"

The Frightening Things looked at each other with terror in their eyes (or in the case of Edgar, eye sockets). After a moment, they nodded in agreement.

"W-we're with you, D-Dinkin," stuttered Arthur, as he shook with fear. "Wherever y-you go, we go ... unless there's a less scary alternative, of course..."

"I wish there was, but there isn't," said Dinkin, gnawing at his fingernails. "Now let's get ready – things are going to get a lot scarier before the night is over..."

LOFTY AMBITIONS

Terrifying shadows: 22
Unwanted inventions: 1
Evil, child-hating creatures
(with a hideous, misshapen claw): ?

Thirty-two minutes later (everyone needed a while to pluck up what little courage they had), Dinkin, Edgar and Herbert were huddled together underneath the loft hatch, with Arthur darting nervously through nearby walls and doors.

"So, I was thinking ... maybe you lot should go first. You know, as a scouting party. I could keep watch from down here..." said Dinkin, as he attached his kneecap-mounted Illu-knee-mators™ (which were basically just bicycle lamps and a lot of sticky tape).

"Oh no you don't, this was your idea!" sniffed Edgar. "We're only doing this so we don't have to be afraid, and we're already terrified! If we're going to face Clawfingers, we'll do it together, or not at all."

"Fine, fine! We'll all go. But everyone stay ghostly, it'll make it harder for Clawfingers to chop us into tiny pieces..." whimpered Dinkin. He stared up at the loft hatch, quaking in his slippers (he still had nine spare pairs), and then linked hands with Herbert. "OK, Arthur ... d-do your stuff." Arthur took Dinkin by the hand, turning everyone ghostly so that they could pass through the loft hatch. As the terrified trio held on tightly, Arthur flew them up into the air...

A second later, Dinkin and the Frightening Things passed through the hatch. Dinkin held his breath, closed his eyes, and tried not to wet his pyjamas in fear. He felt the air go cold, and opened one eye just a crack.

They were in the loft.

Dinkin turned on his Illu-knee-mators™
and pointed his knees into the room. It was
even more terrifying than he could have
imagined! Every corner was jammed with
strange, dusty objects, each one casting
long, sinister shadows across the walls
and floor. The room was filled with piles of
old boxes containing who-knows-what
sinister secrets, mounds of untouched,
unwanted Christmas presents, and stacks of
old newspapers. And somewhere, lurking in
the gloom, was Clawfingers.

"S-stay quiet ... and stay c-connected," stammered a terrified Dinkin, as the ghostly Frightening Things hung on to each other for dear life. "Everybody look out for the old telephone ... oh, and the hideous, child-hating creature with a claw for a hand."

"How will we recognize him?" whispered Arthur.

"Well, if you see someone trying to chop us into tiny pieces, that's probably him," sighed Dinkin, creeping past a coat stand full of his dad's old, foul-smelling fishing jackets that he refused to throw away. "Now keep your eyes peeled, and— AAAAAAAH!"

Dinkin's Illu-knee-mators™ lit up something in the darkness! It was a face! A hideously monstrous face!

"AAAAAAHH! IT'S CLAWFINGERS!" screamed the Frightening Things in unison.

A hysterical Arthur let go of Dinkin and flew into the air. Dinkin and the Frightening Things were solid again! They immediately panicked. Herbert clambered up the coat stand, causing it to topple over on to Edgar, knocking his head off and covering him in a mound of fishy old coats!

"Abort the plan! Arthur, get us out of here!" cried Dinkin. He clambered over a moth-eaten armchair, but his foot went straight through, sending him with a *FWUMP!* on to a pile of boxes marked "OLD GARDEN TOOLS". The tools spilled out all over the floor, and Dinkin was sent skidding through a sea of trowels, forks and spades. Then, as he tried to regain his balance, he stepped on a rake, which flew up with a **PLAM!** into his face.

As he fell to the ground, his Illu-knee-mators™ popped off, skidding to a halt beneath the hideous face. Dinkin stared up in horror.

"A-AAH! It's ... it's..." he began. "Victor?!"

"V-Victor? Who's Victor?" said Herbert, climbing out from underneath the coat stand.

"V.I.C.T.O.R.! The Virtually Indestructible Cybernetic Terror-Obstructor Robot. My first ultimate invention!" said Dinkin, dragging his half-finished invention out of the rubble of forgotten things. The "hideously monstrous" face was in fact just an upside-down dustbin with expressionless eyes and a mouth drawn on it. It was attached to a small vacuum cleaner with a spatula and a wooden spoon taped on to each side to look like arms. The vacuum cleaner hose coiled around it like a long, ridged tail.

"It ... isn't C-Clawfingers?" said Edgar's head from under a particularly stinky coat.

"No, and you can stop panicking, V.I.C.T.O.R. won't hurt us!" said Dinkin, staring at the rather pathetic-looking creation. "Huh ... I guess Dad must have put him up here."

"What does he do?" asked Herbert, giving V.I.C.T.O.R. a prod.

"He doesn't do *anything*. V.I.C.T.O.R. was supposed to protect me from daytime dangers, when you weren't here, but I never got around to finishing him. He probably wouldn't have worked anyway, not without an ultimate invention code. Unless..." he added, spotting the "ON" button on the vacuum cleaner. He pressed it and waited for a moment, but nothing happened. Dinkin shook his head. "Useless! I can't believe I ever thought V.I.C.T.O.R. was the ultimate invention! I mean, look at him – he's nothing but a pile of junk! My new ultimate invention is a million times better than he could ever be!"

"Um, sorry to butt in, but isn't there still the small matter of the gruesome, child-hating monster with the hideous, misshapen claw?" said Edgar, finally reuniting his head with his body.

"AA-AH!" screamed Dinkin, remembering the deadly Clawfingers. "Where's Arthur?"

Suddenly, Arthur appeared out of the box he'd been hiding in and whizzed up into the rafters. He was carrying a small, red object.

"Dinkin, look!" he said. He hovered over Dinkin's head and dropped the object. An old, red telephone landed in Dinkin's hands.

"The telephone! You found it! Now we can input the ultimate invention activation code!" said Dinkin. "Let's get out of here!"

Arthur wasted no time carrying Dinkin and the Frightening Things back to the relative safety of Dinkin's bedroom. Had they stayed a second more, they would have noticed a shape moving in the darkness...

THE ANTI-EVERYTHING MACHINE™

Time: 6:04a.m.
Time spent making ultimate
invention: 4 hours 39 minutes
Time left until everything goes
horribly, horribly wrong: 9 hours
27 minutes

36

For the rest of the night, Dinkin toiled feverishly, gluing, taping and tying his new ultimate invention together. It all took rather a long time, as Dinkin's fear of glue was almost as great as his fear of lofts. He had adapted his De-Randomizing Gloves™ into Glue Grip Gauntlets™ by turning the mittens inside out and adding even more packing tape, but it meant that all the fiddly bits took ages. Meanwhile, the Frightening Things looked on in petrified anticipation.

"I've done it..." whispered Dinkin finally, standing back to admire his creation. "I've *done it*! Behold my indescribably indescribable genius! Behold the one, true ultimate invention! Behold ... the ANTI-EVERYTHING MACHINE™!"

Dinkin stepped aside to reveal a strange small something-or-other. The main part of the machine was made from the lunchbox, which was full to bursting with as many bits and bobs as he could cram into it. The four coaster wheels were attached to the bottom of the box, while the umbrellas were stuck to the side and the aeroplane tail poked out of the back. The TV remote control was taped to the front, and the old telephone was sat on top. It looked, in short, rubbish.

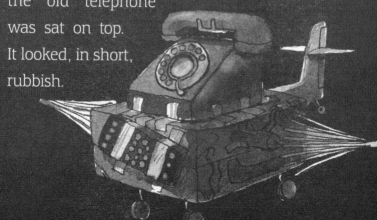

"What ... what does it *do*?" asked Arthur, hovering over it.

"It does everything!" said Dinkin. "Or should I say, *anti*-everything. You see, all this time I've been trying to find ways to avoid everything that's terrifying and horrible ... which is everything! So, since everything is scary, I realized I had to get rid of everything!"

"Get rid of ... *everything*?" repeated Herbert, chewing nervously on the corner of Dinkin's duvet. "Won't that leave *nothing*?"

"Exactly! That's the genius of the Anti-Everything Machine™! There'll be nothing to fear! Nothing to be afraid of! Nothing at all!" said Dinkin. He took a piece of paper out of his pyjama pocket and unfolded it. Then he unfolded it again. And again. Written on the paper was a number. It was 986 digits long. "This is the ultimate invention activation code, or as I like to call it, the Anti-Everything Code. All I have to do is dial this number into the telephone, and *VOILA!* No more everything!"

"Oh dear, oh dear…" said Edgar. "Dinkin, are you absolutely sure this is a good idea? I mean … do you really want to get rid of *everything*?"

"Yeah, doesn't everything include this room? The whole house? Even your mum and dad?" said Herbert.

"And what about us? Do *we* count as everything? What's going to happen to us?" squealed Arthur, flying anxiously around the lamp like a hypnotized moth.

"Well, no, I mean ... maybe, I mean, I don't know..." began Dinkin, suddenly a bit unsure what the Anti-Everything Machine™ was actually going to do. "But it's my only chance to never be scared again!" he said.

"But it seems so very *final*..." said Edgar, his bones creaking with fear. "Are you really sure about turning it on? I think I speak for all of us when I say ... oh no, we're vanishing!"

"What?" said Dinkin. He looked at the Frightening Things. It was true – as the dawn light crept into the room, they began to fade.

"Oh Dinkin, don't do anything rash – at least wait until tonight..." said Edgar, and a second later they had disappeared, leaving Dinkin alone with his ultimate invention. He stared at the Anti-Everything Code for a moment, doubt creeping into his brain. Could the Frightening Things have a point? Was getting rid of everything a step too far, no matter how terrifying it was? Finally, he made up his mind.

"They don't know what they're talking about. This is the only way," he said. He picked up the Anti-Everything Machine™, and was just preparing to dial the first number into the telephone when there was a knock at his door. It was his mother.

"Morning, Dinkin, up already? Oh, good! That gives you plenty of time to get ready for school..."

NIGHTMARE DAY

Fear of green shoes:
3.2.1.4 KiloScares
Fear of maths test:
5.5.6.8 KiloScares
Fear of nightmares:
9.9.9.8 KiloScares

42 Dinkin did his best to convince his mother that it was in the interests of everyone that he entered the 986 digit number into the Anti-Everything Machine™ before he went to school, but she simply wasn't having it.

"You can play with your new toy when you get home. It's not as though it's going anywhere," she said.

"It's not a toy! It's the Anti-Everything Machine™!" Dinkin protested.

"And it'll still be here when you get back," said Mrs Dings, shuffling him into the bathroom. "Honestly, Dinkin, I hope you haven't been up all night again – you'll fall asleep in class at this rate..."

Before he left for school, an exhausted Dinkin covered the Anti-Everything Machine™ with the Complete Concealment Cover-Up Cover™ and hid the Anti-Everything Code under his mattress.

"I'll be back soon," he whispered to his ultimate invention. "And then everything must go..."

On the bus, Dinkin thought of nothing else but the Anti-Everything Machine™, but he was so tired after a night of invention-making that he could barely stay awake. He didn't even notice that Gilbert G. Gilbertson was wearing worryingly green shoes (green being the second scariest colour after orange), or that Boris Wack was eating crisps in a moving vehicle (a Crisp Crumb Crisis in the making), or any other of the supremely scary things that were happening all around him. He didn't even hear Misty Spittle call him "Dinkin dumb-pants", which usually made him think that his underwear was secretly draining his brainpower (he had already thrown away eighteen pairs of underpants for that very reason). In fact, he was so tired that he barely even flinched when Ms Feebleback announced a "surprise" maths test. It was all he could do to keep his eyes open.

"Must ... turn on ... Anti-Everything Machine™..." mumbled a delirious Dinkin as Ms Feebleback handed out the last of the test papers. "Must ... make everything ... *anti*-everything..."

"No talking!" snapped Ms Feebleback. This was the last thing Dinkin remembered. A wave of tiredness washed over him, and he felt his eyelids begin to close. Before long, he had slipped into a deep sleep...

DINKIN, WAKE UP, said a voice from out of nowhere.

"Hmm? What?" said Dinkin, opening his eyes. Oddly, Dinkin wasn't in the classroom any more. In fact, he wasn't *anywhere*. All around him was nothingness. Nothing but nothingness.

"AAAAAH!" he screamed. "Where am I? Where is everything?!" He immediately looked around for something to hide behind, but there was nothing there. There was nothing anywhere! "Help! HELP! Where am I?"

45

There's nowhere to hide, said the voice from out of nowhere. In fact, there's nowhere at all.

"AAA-AAA-AHH!" screamed Dinkin again. "Mum! Dad! HELP!"

Don't bother calling for them, Dinkin Dings. They don't exist, thanks to you! laughed the voice.

"AAAA-AA-AAAH!" screamed Dinkin for a third time (of four). He fell to his knees and tried to summon the Frightening Things.

Frightening Things, Frightening Things,
Creep from the gloom,
Crawl from the shadows and—

The Frightening Things can't help you – they don't exist either! said the voice.

You turned on the Anti-Everything Machine™. "Everything must go", you said, and so everything went!

"No, I didn't turn it on! I didn't have time! At least I don't think I did ... did I? Oh no! Did I? I didn't mean to! I thought it was for the best! Make everything come back!" cried Dinkin, closing his eyes tightly.

Too late … you're all that's left now! said the voice from out of nowhere.

"No! It can't be! It can't!"

Oh, but it is! All that's left … is Dinkin Dings! said the voice.

"AAAAAAA-AAAA-AHHHH!" screamed Dinkin for the fourth and final time (in this chapter, anyway). It almost drowned out the sound of the voice shouting,

All that's left is DINKIN DINGS! DINKIN DINGS! DINKIN DINGS!

"Dinkin Dings!" said a strangely familiar voice. "Are you asleep?" It was Ms Feebleback! Dinkin woke up with a start – he'd just had a nightmare!

"What? No! Everything's gone! Nothing left except ... me!" he rambled feverishly.

"Honestly, Dinkin, this is simply not acceptable behaviour. I know maths is boring – I mean, *everyone* knows that – but you don't see anyone else trying to sleep through the test, do you?" said Ms Feebleback.

Dinkin's eyes darted around the classroom as he started to panic. How could he have been so blind? The Frightening Things had been right all along – his nightmare proved it. His ultimate invention was just too terrifying to ever be used! He had been so close to ending everything that it sent a shiver down his spine and made his eyes water. He had no choice – he had to destroy the Anti-Everything Machine™ as soon as possible. But then Dinkin had another thought:

What if the Anti-Everything Machine™ fell into the wrong hands? It would be the end of everything – and it'd be all my fault!

Dinkin shuddered with fear. He had created a monster, and he had to destroy it, no matter the cost. But first, he needed an incredibly, impossibly ingenious plan to get out of the classroom. He thought for a moment, and then put up his hand.

"Please, Ms Feebleback, can I go to the toilet?"

THE GREAT ESCAPE

Pigeon peril at 26%
Haunting hazard at 68%
Invention tension at 92%

It was the third time that week that Dinkin had used Escape Route FOUR-FOUR-FOUR to save himself from a hideous fate:

Monday – to get out of eating Mrs Hogjaw's toxic, stomach-melting "meat" pie (Dinkin wasn't sure if minced slugs counted as meat, but he was absolutely sure they were the main ingredient).

Tuesday – to escape The Assault of the Evil Killer Cosmic Cloud from the Evil Killer Cosmos, which was about to engulf the entire school. Or it might have been a spot of rain – Dinkin couldn't be sure.

Thursday (today) – to get home and dismantle his all-new Anti-Everything Machine™ before someone turned it on and put an end to everything.

Dinkin rushed into the toilet, opened the window and was just climbing on to the ledge when...

"What are you doing?" said a voice.

"AAAAAH!" screamed Dinkin. He turned round to see the smallest boy in class 5D, Roddy Jollify, standing at the sink with yet another nosebleed.

"Are you skiving school? You'll never get out that way, it's too high," said Roddy, as he pushed a wad of tissue up his nostril.

"D-don't distract me – this is m-more terrifying than it looks!" said Dinkin pulling himself up on to the ledge.

He looked down at the bushes below. It was a far enough drop that he'd hurt himself if he fell, and Dinkin wasn't good with heights (or widths or depths). But there was no turning back. He held his breath, and jumped...

"AAAAA" – POING!

Dinkin landed in the bush – and bounced back out again on to the grass! Roddy hurried to the window. There was a trampoline hidden in the bushes! Written in big black letters on top of the trampoline were the words DO NOT REMOVE FROM THE SCHOOL GYM, followed by, THAT MEANS YOU, DINKIN DINGS!

"I'm telling on you!" shouted Roddy, but Dinkin was already at the school gates. Now, even though he'd made it out, there were a hundred horrifying obstacles to get past before he could get to the Anti-Everything Machine™ and dismantle it. The worst of these were:

CARS

PIGEONS

PIGEONS DRIVING CARS (Dinkin hadn't actually seen this first-hand, but it made a scary sense the two would go together)

UNEVEN PAVING SLABS

UNEVEN NUMBERS (Dinkin didn't like to call them "odd numbers" in case they were offended and came after him. Nevertheless, he couldn't look at the sign for 99p Bon-Bon Bags in Mr Sweet's House of Unsavoury Treats without breaking into a cold sweat)

HATS (especially berets)

CLOUDS (obviously)

and SPACE-DINOSAURS

With so much to worry about, it was all Dinkin could do to put one foot in front of the other, but the thought of the Anti-Everything Machine™ falling into evil hands filled him with an even greater fear. He ran without stopping until he got home – almost. As he arrived at the old playground he held his breath and slowed to a terrified tip-toe. Playgrounds were scary enough, but Dinkin was convinced that this particular playground was haunted. The swings and roundabouts seemed to creak and move all on their own, as if being ridden by ghosts who couldn't get off.

Indeed, it was one of the first places Dinkin had ever been scared of, and was still firmly in his "Top 100 Terrors".

Dinkin knew his mum and dad would both be at work by now, so when he arrived home he took the key from under the mat and let himself in. The moment he entered the house, he caught a faint smell of fish, but he was so worried about the Anti-Everything Machine™ that he didn't even think about it – he just dashed straight upstairs. He was almost at the top when he stopped in his tracks and looked up.

The loft hatch was open.

Dinkin froze, numb with terror. Why was it open? It couldn't be his dad – no one was home! Was it someone getting in ... or someone getting *out*?

Every last bit of him wanted to run downstairs and out of the house and never stop. But the only thing more terrifying than a mysteriously open loft hatch was the thought of someone turning on the Anti-Everything Machine™. Dinkin closed his eyes, held his breath, and ran past the hatch to his room. The door was ajar. He was almost too afraid to look, and had a scream ready just in case the Anti-Everything Machine™ was gone.

"AAA—" he began, but there, on the desk, was the Anti-Everything Machine™, covered in the Complete Concealment Cover-Up Cover™, just like he'd left it! Dinkin breathed such an enormous sigh of relief that he almost fainted. "It's safe...!" he whispered to himself, almost as relieved as he was terrified, but then he looked again. Something didn't look quite right, but he couldn't put his finger on it. He nervously approached the table. He reached out a shaking hand, held his breath and lifted the cover.

"WA-AAA-AHH!" he screamed! It wasn't the Anti-Everything Machine™ at all – it was a piece of cardboard, chopped roughly into its shape! His ultimate invention was gone! Dinkin staggered backwards, staring in horror at the cut-out. Where was his machine? His head began to spin as his eyes darted around the room. It was then that he saw it.

Three deep claw marks, running down the wall. And below, five words, scratched into the wallpaper.

IT'S MY ULTIMATE
INVENTION NOW

"AAA-A-AAAAH!!!" screamed Dinkin!

The wallpaper was ruined!

Oh yes, and Clawfingers was on the loose, and he'd stolen the Anti-Everything Machine™.

"AAA-AA-AAAA-AAAAAAAH!!!"

THE FORTRESS OF COMPLETE AND UTTER PROTECTION

Cardboard boxes used to build
fortress: 6
Rolls of sticky tape used to
secure fortress: 23
Times fortress has survived the
end of the world (so far): 0

Dinkin rushed straight into his new, improved
Fortress of Complete and Utter Protection. He
closed the Drawbridge of Absolutely-No-
Entry-Whatsoever-and-I-Really-Mean-It-This-
Time-Ness, and sealed the Door of Definite
Defence. There were so many things to be
scared of that Dinkin didn't know where to
start. Was Clawfingers still in the house? Was
he planning on turning on the Anti-
Everything Machine™? Would his mum and
dad believe that it wasn't he who had ruined
the wallpaper? Dinkin huddled in a corner of

the fortress and waited for the end of everything – or something even worse.

And he waited. And waited.

And waited a little bit more.

After three hours and fifty-eight minutes, Dinkin started to wonder if the end of everything had happened already, but he just hadn't heard it. He nervously pushed open the fortress's Window Incognito (a small hole in the cardboard that Dinkin could look out of via a system of mirrors) and peeked out. He was met with two bespectacled eyes.

"Dink! What's all this? I pop back to get my lunch and what do I find? The loft hatch open and you, home from school in the middle of the day! What on earth's going on?"

After Dinkin had stopped screaming, he realized that it was his dad looking back at him. In one breath, he said:

"Dad, I did a terrible thing, I built an Anti-Everything Machine™ so that everything would stop being scary, but then I fell asleep in the maths test and I had a dream that everything would be even more scary if I actually activated the machine 'cause there wouldn't be anything and I'd be all alone and there wouldn't be you or Mum or the Frightening Things or ANYTHING and then I used Escape Route FOUR-FOUR-FOUR to escape and ran all the way home (except past the old playground) and when I got here everything was OK and the Anti-Everything Machine™ was here, but then I realized it wasn't the Anti-Everything Machine™

because the actual Anti-Everything Machine™ has been stolen by Clawfingers!"

Dinkin's dad nodded thoughtfully for a moment, adjusted his glasses, then looked around.

"Well, everything seems to be OK now," he said. "Why don't you come out from there?"

"No way! I'm never coming out!" said Dinkin. "This is the only probably slightly safe place left in the world!"

"Dink, I'm sure everything's – oh, no!" said Mr Dings.

"What? *What?*" squealed Dinkin, panicking.

"You've ruined the wallpaper!" said Dinkin's dad, noticing the wall. "Dink, what did your mother and I say about writing on things that aren't meant to be written on?"

Dinkin did have a habit of writing where he shouldn't. He often drew symbols on his wall to repel vampires, werewolves and vampire-werewolves, and he'd once painted the words DON'T LAND HERE on the front lawn to discourage lazy aeroplane pilots from crash-landing on his house. All of which made Mr Dings more than a little suspicious about the writing on the wall.

"What? No! That wasn't me!" cried Dinkin. "It was Clawfingers! He came down from the loft! He could still be in the house!"

"Claw who? Oh, not that loft-monster you're always going on about! How many times do I have to tell you, Dinkin, *there is no Clawfingers*. There's nothing to be afraid of in the loft, and there never has been. Now come out of there – you can't stay in a box for ever," sighed Mr Dings, although he wasn't sure he believed it. Dinkin could hide away in his cardboard fortress for *ages*. His top three hide-outs were:

1) THREAT: SKY FALLING IN
(DURATION OF STAY: 8 HOURS)
2) THREAT: INVASION OF VULTURE
MEN FROM VENUS
(DURATION OF STAY: 10 HOURS)
3) THREAT: VISIT FROM GRANDMA
DINGS (DURATION OF STAY: 22½ HOURS)

Indeed, no amount of coaxing could get Dinkin to leave. He was still in there when his mum came home and assured him that Clawfingers wasn't lying in wait for him. He was still in there when his dad pushed a bowl of macaroni (and his pyjamas) through the Window Incognito. And he was still there when his parents finally gave up on trying to get him out and went to bed. Dinkin looked at his watch, willing the hands towards midnight.

This was a job for the Frightening Things! Again!

THE AUNTIE
EVERYDAY CODE

Time: 12:02
"Dinkin" time: two minutes
past "AAaAH!"

Although the Frightening Things appeared almost immediately, it took a good minute and thirty-two seconds for them to realize where Dinkin was.

"In here!" said Dinkin, opening the door (even Arthur couldn't pass through the Door of Definite Defence). They huddled together in the fortress as Dinkin explained his dilemma.

"If Clawfingers turns on the machine, the world will start to get sucked into it! Before long there'll be nothing left but me … just like in my nightmare!"

"Perhaps ... perhaps Clawfingers doesn't *want* to destroy everything," said Arthur, hopefully. "Perhaps he was trying to stop *you* from destroying everything! After all, if he was going to do it, wouldn't he have done it by now?"

"Well, it'd take him a while to enter all those numbers anyway, especially with that hideous, misshapen claw of his..." said Herbert, starting to chew on the fortress control panel.

"What numbers?" asked Dinkin.

"The numbers on your piece of paper," replied Herbert. "You know, the, um, Auntie Everyday Code."

"The Anti-Everything Code!" screamed Dinkin. "I forgot all about it – it's still under my mattress!"

Dinkin and the Frightening Things crept out of the fortress, each one more terrified than the last. While the Frightening Things kept watch for signs of everything-ending-ness, Dinkin nervously reached his hand under his mattress. There was the piece of paper, folded up just where he'd left it.

"It's still here! It's OK!" he cried in relief. "Clawfingers can't turn on the Anti-Everything Machine™ without the Anti-Everything Code!"

"So, what do we do now?" said Edgar, his bones rattling with fear.

"We have to destroy the code, it's the only way to be safe," said Dinkin, his mind racing. After a moment, he spotted Herbert picking a bit of slipper out of his teeth. "That's it! Here, Herbert – *eat this.*"

"Who, me? No way! I can't eat a piece of paper," moaned Herbert. "I have a very sensitive stomach."

"You ate my slippers!" cried Dinkin. "I've seen you eat pens, soap – even a toilet seat!"

"You don't like peas, and I don't like paper," said Herbert, crossing his scaly arms stubbornly.

"Peas are rolled-up beetles in disguise! Everyone knows that!" cried Dinkin. "Paper is just ... oh, this is getting us nowhere. We'll have to think of some other way."

As quickly and fearfully as they could, Dinkin and the Frightening Things tried to work out the best way of destroying the Anti-Everything Code. The shortlist was:

1) TELEPORT IT INTO ANOTHER DIMENSION (obstacle to success of plan – no teleportation device)

2) DE-MOLECULARIZE IT (obstacle to success of plan – no de-molecularizer)

3) CUT IT INTO TINY PIECES (obstacle to success of plan – Dinkin's terrible fear of scissors)

4) TEAR IT INTO TINY PIECES (obstacle to success of plan – Dinkin's terrible fear of paper cuts)

69

Finally, they decided to bury the Anti-Everything Code in the back garden, and let the worms make a meal of it. It wasn't ideal, but when everyone making the decision is scared of everything, getting any sort of agreement is tricky. They crossed their fingers, bones and claws and made their way downstairs...

THE RISE OF CLAWFINGERS

Terror at 9.8.6.2 KiloScares
and rising

Dinkin and the Frightening Things tiptoed down the stairs and into the hall, then crept into the kitchen, where Dinkin found a spoon for digging in the garden.

"No time to invent the Earth Turf 2000™ – this will have to do," said Dinkin, examining the spoon. "Right, everyone stay close behind me ... and no screaming."

"You can rely on us, Dinkin," said Arthur. "Apart from the no screaming part, obviously."

Dinkin reached the back door and began unlocking the nine different locks, bolts and chains that he insisted his parents fit, then made his way nervously out into the garden. He immediately wished he hadn't left his Illu-knee-mators™ in the loft. It was almost pitch dark, and cold enough to make him shiver, even if he wasn't already trembling with fear. The moonlight made everything look three and a half times more haunted than normal. In the distance, an owl hooted as if to say, "It's the end of everything!" Dinkin crept slowly out into the middle of the lawn, then took the Anti-Everything Code from his pocket and started to dig as the Frightening Things huddled behind him.

"Who's got the torch? It's too dark to see," he said. "Someone turn on the light."

The next moment, a bright light shone on to the ground.

"Thanks," said Dinkin.

"Wasn't me," said Herbert.

"Or me," said Arthur.

"Well, I didn't do it," said Edgar.

Suddenly, Dinkin caught a faint whiff of stale fish in the air. He turned around slowly, his eyes wide with terror. A massive shape loomed over the Frightening Things, its eyes burning like fire.

"You OK, Dinkin? You like you've seen a ghost," said Arthur.

"C-C-C— " began Dinkin.

"Could you lend a hand? Can't believe we're doing this? Cold, isn't it?" said Edgar, trying to guess what Dinkin wanted to say.

"C-CLAWFINGERS!" screamed Dinkin.
The Frightening Things turned around.
"AAA-AAAAA-AAA-AAAH!"

Standing on the lawn was the most terrifying creature they had ever seen! He was more terrifying than a dozen man-eating Fish-Men, or a whole spaceship-full of Flesh-eating Alien Space Zombies From Beyond Terror! The enormous creature was hunched and malformed, and a tattered, old coat (which smelled rather like stale fish) hung off his body like loose skin. He wore a cardboard box as a mask (presumably because it was so terrifyingly monstrous) and his glowing eyes shone like lanterns through cut-out holes. He only had one arm, which ended in a foul, misshapen three-fingered claw.

"Dinkin ... Dings..." growled Clawfingers in a voice that sounded like nails scraping down a blackboard (at the same time that a cat was being strangled). He lifted his one arm and waved his hideous, misshapen claw.

"Ruh – ruh – ruh— " Dinkin began.

"Ruuuuun!" screamed the Frightening Things, scattering in all directions. Dinkin grabbed the code and ran after them.

"Dinkin ... Dings..." growled Clawfingers again, lumbering after him and swinging his claw! Dinkin dashed back into the house, but by the time Herbert and Edgar had scrambled through the back door, Clawfingers was almost upon them. Dinkin tried to push the door shut, but Clawfingers lunged against it!

"Help me!" cried Dinkin. "He's going to chop me into little pieces! Or worse!"

Herbert and Edgar threw themselves at the door, but it was no good – Clawfingers forced his way inside and started swinging his claw around!

"AAAA-AAA-AAH!" screamed Dinkin and the Frightening Things.

"Back to the fortress!" cried Dinkin. "It's our only chance!"

As Dinkin and the Frightening Things raced out of the kitchen, Clawfingers lumbered around, swinging his claw into cupboards (**KWUD!**) and chairs (**KRUD!**) as he chased after them.

"Dinkin ... Dings..." bellowed the claw-fingered creature.

"There's no Dinkin Dings here! You've got the wrong house! Dinkin lives next door!" squealed Dinkin, as they

raced towards the stairs. Unfortunately, Herbert tripped over his tail and crashed to the floor, narrowly missing Mr Ding's cabinet of fishing trophies.

"Herbert!" shouted Dinkin. He dragged Herbert to his feet just as Clawfingers lurched towards them. He was right on top of them! Clawfingers swung his claw again, missing Dinkin's head by a millimetre and smashing the cabinet into pieces!

CRA-ASH!

"Go! Go! GO!" Dinkin screamed, dragging Herbert with him as he scrambled past Clawfingers. They dashed up the stairs, with the creature shambling after them. Dinkin raced into his room and dived into the fortress. He waited for the Frightening Things to fly, scramble and clatter their way in, then he slammed the drawbridge shut and locked the door.

"He'll skin us alive!" shouted Edgar.

"He'll chop us into pieces!" cried Arthur.

"He'll ... he'll ... actually, I can't think of anything worse than that..." added Herbert.

"ShhHH!" said Dinkin. "He'll hear us!"

Everyone clamped their hands over their mouths and waited for what seemed like twenty-four seconds (it was only twenty-two).

Dinkin held his breath as the footsteps got closer, and prayed that he would spontaneously explode rather than face the fury of Clawfingers. The light went on, then he heard a knock at the drawbridge.

"You in there, Dink?"

"D-D-Dad?" said Dinkin, opening the Window Incognito just a fraction.

"What's going on? We can't sleep a wink with you making such an awful racket. Don't you think it's time you stopped messing around and went to bed?"

"Dad, get Mum! Into the fortress, quick! Clawfingers is in the house!"

"Who?" yawned Dinkin's mum, as she shambled into his bedroom.

Dinkin tried to explain, but neither of them were "in any mood for silliness".

"But Clawfingers is real! I saw him! So did the Frightening Things!" said Dinkin from inside the fortress. Mr and Mrs Dings looked at each other.

"And are the 'Frightening Things' with you right now?" said Dinkin's mum, shaking her head.

"Of course they are! You don't think I'd wander round the house at night on my own, do you?" said Dinkin, frantically.

"Fair point, I suppose," sighed Mr Dings. "But will you please try and keep the noise down? Your mum and I are trying to sleep!"

"It's not safe out there! Into the fortress, quick – the Frightening Things will budge up!" said Dinkin.

"Dink, you're being silly again … super silly," said Mr Dings.

"Super-duper silly!" added Mrs Dings.

"Sillier than Super-Duper Silly Man, the silliest superhero in Sillytown," giggled Mr Dings. Dinkin shook his head. What was it going to take for them to believe him?

"Now you may have the day off tomorrow, but some of us have to work at the weekend," said Dinkin's dad. "So let's have no more nonsense about this 'Clawfingers'. It's way past all our bedtimes."

"'Night, Dinkin … I'll leave the lights on and the door open just in case," said Mrs Dings.

"Oh yes, brilliant idea, leave the lights on. That should stop the bloodthirsty claw-handed maniac…" sighed Dinkin.

MR DINGS VS. THE FORTRESS

Mr Dings:
65% water, 18.5% carbon,
9.5% hydrogen, 7% "smackdown"
Fortress:
4% impenetrable
96% cardboard

Dinkin didn't sleep a wink for the second night running. The thought of Clawfingers on the loose, and with the Anti-Everything Machine™, was almost too terrifying to contemplate. Did Clawfingers know about the Anti-Everything Code? Had he heard Dinkin talking about it through the ceiling? If he got his claws on the code, he would almost certainly turn on the machine and that would be that for everything. For now, the Anti-Everything Code was still safely in his pocket, but how long before Clawfingers found a way to get to the code and bring Dinkin's nightmare to life?

"Good luck today, Dinkin – try not to get chopped into a million pieces," said Edgar, as the morning light shone through the Window Incognito.

"Thanks..." muttered Dinkin, as the Frightening Things began to fade. Within moments, they were gone.

Six seconds later, there was a knock on the top of the fortress.

"AAAAH— " began Dinkin.

"Dinkin, it's your father," said Dinkin's dad, in a much firmer voice than normal. "I've just seen the state of the kitchen, and the hall ... and my fishing cabinet! I notice you failed to mention last night that you'd smashed it to bits!"

"That wasn't me, that was Clawfingers! I did try to explain, but you wouldn't listen," said Dinkin.

"Clawfingers again? What did I tell you

about using the 'C' word in this house?!" said Dinkin's dad, more sternly than Dinkin had ever heard him. "Now come out of that 'fortress' at once!"

"Not a chance! I have to keep the Anti-Everything Code safe! If Clawfingers gets it, he'll destroy everything! I really thought I'd explained this..." said a frustrated Dinkin.

"Dinkin Danger Dings, I am your father, and I insist you come out of there this second! I shall count to three. One..."

Dinkin heard his mother saying, "Oh, Mr Dings, don't do anything rash..."

"Two..." said Dinkin's dad.

"Oh dear," said Dinkin's mum.

"'Oh dear' what?" said Dinkin.

"THREE!" cried Dinkin's dad, and ripped the drawbridge off its hinges like it was a piece of cardboard! Dinkin watched in horror as his dad pulled the roof off the fortress, then tore the walls to pieces with his bare hands! How was it possible? Was the fortress destabilized by inter-galactic weather conditions? Was his dad (as he had often suspected) a super-powerful Mandroid from the year 10,012 with the ability to control all technology? Whatever the reason, it took under a minute for his dad to rip his Fortress of Complete and Utter Protection to shreds. Dinkin cowered amongst the wreckage of his not-so-impenetrable stronghold, completely defenceless against Clawfingers.

"There, that's better! Now that you've got nowhere to hide, perhaps you'll realize that there's really nothing to be scared of!" said Dinkin's dad, still fuming. "Now then, I am going to spend my whole Saturday in the office, because some of us have work to do, and can't just sit around all day panicking about everything!"

"Work...?" said Dinkin, an idea hitting him like a runaway train (which also made him nervous about being hit by an actual runaway train). "You're going to work? I'd ... I'd love to see where you work, Dad!"

"Really?" said Dinkin's dad, suddenly brightening up. "You want to see where I work?"

"I do, I really, really do," said Dinkin, crossing his fingers. Of course, the thought of going anywhere near an office was so terrifying that it made Dinkin shake uncontrollably. But he knew that if he was going to protect the Anti-Everything Code, sacrifices would have to be made. For he had seen the future … and it was terrifying.

OFFICE OF HORRORS

Number of lifts: 1
Number of stairs: 160

Dinkin's dad was so delighted that Dinkin wanted to see where he worked that he immediately agreed to take him along. As he drove to the office with Dinkin at his side, he was positively giddy with excitement.

"This is going to be great! You can see where I keep my pens, the fridge where I keep my sandwiches, and you can even sit at my desk! There's so much to do," he said, as they pulled into a large car park. A huge, grey building loomed over them like a giant encased in concrete. Dinkin checked the

Anti-Everything Code was safe in his pocket for the eighty-third time that morning and followed his dad into the building. Everything about the lobby was only mildly horrifying (the security guard was definitely a robot, and all the pot plants looked distinctly man-eating) – until they reached the lift.

"Hop in, Dink, it's a quick ride to the top," said his dad, cheerfully.

Dinkin was desperate to get as far away as possible from Clawfingers, but there was no way he was riding in a lift (or "bungee box" as he called it), which was Number Three on his list of 114 Most Totally Terrifying Methods of Transportation (after horses and bicycles).

Dinkin's dad took one look at the expression of horror on Dinkin's face and sighed. "We'll take the stairs," he said.

Eight flights later, Dinkin and his dad reached the top. Dinkin was about to search for a decent hiding place when a tiny old lady with alarmingly thick glasses ran up to him, squealing with excitement.

"It can't be! Is this little Duncan?" she said, peering at Dinkin.

"Hello ... Gillian..." panted Mr Dings, as he tried to catch his breath. "Yes, this is Dinkin – see, I told you he was real! Dinkin, say hello to Gillian from accounts."

"Duncan! Aren't you the cutest! I could just eat you up!" squealed Gillian, ruffling Dinkin's hair.

Dinkin couldn't believe it! The one place he thought he might be safe from Clawfingers, and now an old woman was threatening to eat him! And it didn't stop there. Mr Dings dragged Dinkin around the office, showing him off to anyone he could find. Dinkin wasn't sure any of them were genuinely human. His initial impressions were:

Man with beard – werewolf

Short man with odd socks – mutant

Unsettlingly tall woman with wig (or hair that looks like wig) – gut-sucking, interdimensional ghoul-witch

By the time they got to his dad's desk, Dinkin was even more nervous at the thought of staying in the office, but he had no choice. He had to keep the Anti-Everything Code as far away from Clawfingers as possible.

"Why don't you sit up here on my chair – you can pretend to be a grown-up!" said Mr Dings, cheerfully. "I've got to go to a meeting, but I won't be long. Just ... please behave yourself until I get back..."

"But ... but..." protested Dinkin as his dad hoisted him on to his chair and hurried to his meeting. Dinkin tapped his pocket again. He reached in and took out the Anti-Everything Code, and stared at it in the hope that he would think of an ingenious, non-terrifying way of destroying it. After a moment, however, he realized that the paper smelled rather strange. Strange, and familiar. He leaned towards it slightly and sniffed.

It smelled like stale fish.

Dinkin froze. He stared down, unblinking, at the paper in his hand. Finally, he dared to unfold it, and looked down. There was no 986 number code on the paper at all. Instead, it said (in very bad handwriting):

> NOW I'VE GOT THE ANTI-
> EVERYTHING CODE, TOO.

Below it, in smaller (but equally bad) writing was:

> I HAVE TOYED WITH YOU ENOUGH.
> COME TO THE OLD PLAYGROUND AT
> MIDNIGHT, AND COME ALONE. THE
> FATE OF EVERYTHING DEPENDS ON IT.
>   SINCERELY,
>   CLAWFINGERS
>
>   P.S. SORRY ABOUT MY HANDWRITING,
> IT'S TRICKY TO WRITE WITH THIS
> HIDEOUS, MISSHAPEN CLAW OF MINE.
>   SEE YOU AT MIDNIGHT!
>
>   (I'LL BE THE ONE WITH THE
> HIDEOUS, MISSHAPEN CLAW)

Well, obviously, thought Dinkin.

SHOWDOWN AT MIDNIGHT

Chances of Dinkin going
to bed early: 89.35%
Chances of Dinkin going
to meet Clawfingers: 89.486%
Chances of Dinkin having
a go on the see-saw: 0.42%

Dinkin was easily ten times more terrified than he had ever been before as he waited for his meeting with Clawfingers. The rest of the day passed in a blur, and he didn't mutter a single word until he got home. Then, in the middle of dinner, just as Mr Dings was explaining for the eleventh time how great it was to take Dinkin to work with him, Dinkin finally spoke.

"I've got it – I've worked it out!" he cried.

"Worked what out, Dink?" asked his dad.

"A way to save everything! Maybe..." he said. He didn't have time to explain further –

and anyway, he didn't want to be told how "stupendously silly" he was being. He raced around the house, collecting everything he needed. After one minute and forty-eight seconds, he had collected:

1 bottle cap

and

1 marker pen

Dinkin raced to his room and started work. Two hours and seven minutes later, the Invention Prevention Addition was complete. Dinkin stared at the clock.

19:48

It was still quite early, so he sat down on his bed and panicked about the end of everything until:

23:33

...by which time Mr and Mrs Dings had gone to bed, leaving Dinkin alone. He carried on counting the minutes until it was time to go, and then quickly wrote a note to the Frightening Things:

> Gone to meet Clawfingers
> at old playground.
> Must try to save everything.
> And not get chopped into
> little pieces.
> PLEASE HELP!!!
> Lots of love, Dinkin x

He put on his coat over his pyjamas and slid his feet into his slippers. He climbed carefully out of his window (a slightly-less-daring version of Escape Route SEVEN-ZERO-SEVEN) and wandered fearfully down the street in the cold night air.

"D-d-don't p-panic, Dinkin," he whispered to himself. "It'll all b-be over s-soon, one way or another..."

Dinkin arrived at the playground at 23:38. He made his way nervously inside and waited. He looked around, but he couldn't see anyone. All he could see was a terrifying array of deadly rides:

See-Saw
(the perfect
instrument of torture
for two people. Even if
you don't want to join in,
you have to, and as far as Dinkin could
see, once you're on it, it's impossible to
get off) 3.5.2.8 KiloScares

(Dinkin didn't have his Threat-O-Meter™
with him, so he had to estimate the readings)

Swings (held together
entirely with rust and the
willpower of whoever is
crazy enough to get on
them.) 6.6.6.1 KiloScares

Slide (which
made you move more
quickly than any human
being should, even if you
hung on to the
sides) 8.8.9.8
KiloScares

Dinkin couldn't think of a worse place for a just-before-midnight showdown. He looked at his watch ... (23:40) and carried on waiting ... (23:44) ... and waiting ... (23:58).

After a while he wondered if the creature was coming at all – maybe he was just going to put an end to everything and be done with it. This might even be a trick, to get Dinkin out of the house! Panic gripped him like a misshapen claw around his neck. He checked his watch again.

00:01

Clawfingers was late!

Then, four seconds later, Dinkin realized something else.

It was after midnight – he could summon the Frightening Things! He'd never tried to summon them from this far away before, but it was his only chance. He started to back out of the playground (to get a better "summoning signal") and began the Ancient Summoning Chant:

"Frightening Things, Frightening Things,
Creep from the gloom,
Crawl from the shadows and into my room,
Frightening Things, Frightening Things,
Come to my aid,
Save me from danger (and being af — "
DUMF!

He backed into something! Dinkin froze, hoping that it might be a climbing frame or swing. It was then he smelled that familiar smell of stale fish, and turned his head, slowly. He was met with two glowing eyes, and a hideous, misshapen claw. The creature leaned towards him, and spoke:

"Dinkin
... Dings..."

THE SECRET OF CLAWFINGERS

Chances of Clawfingers
having a secret: 100%
Chances of Dinkin working
it out: 1%

"Dinkin ... Dings ... wait, it is you, isn't it? It's so hard to see in this thing. I mean, with these eyes ... I mean..." said Clawfingers, suddenly sounding just slightly less terrifying than the last time they met. He pointed his lamp-like eyes right in Dinkin's face. "Oh good! You look even more scared than last night in the garden. Turns out I really am quite good at this terrifying business! You'd never know I'd only been doing it for two days..."

"T-t-two days..?" stuttered Dinkin.

"What? No, I mean, ages! Years! For ever! I've always been Clawfingers!" said Clawfingers quickly, and waved his claw in Dinkin's face.

"Please don't chop me into little pieces..." said Dinkin in his most terror-filled whimper.

"Yes, well, we'll see about that. I haven't made up my mind about the chopping," said Clawfingers. "Or about turning on *this*."

He reached deep inside his coat with his claw ... and pulled out the Anti-Everything Machine!™

"Don't try anything," said Clawfingers. "I've entered 985 of the 986 numbers of the Anti-Everything Code into the telephone. All I have to do is dial '0' and it's 'goodbye' to everything!"

"Please, don't!" begged Dinkin. "You don't understand – it'll mean the end of everything! You can't turn it on!"

"But that's exactly what you were going to do, wasn't it? You thought your ultimate invention would be the answer to everything..." said Clawfingers.

"I hadn't thought it through! The end of everything would be rubbish! I'd rather things were the way they are!" said Dinkin, looking around to see if there was any sign of the Frightening Things.

"So ... you might say this isn't your ultimate invention, after all?" said Clawfingers.

"No, no! It's my worst invention ever! I wish I'd never built it!" said Dinkin, desperately.

"Good! Then perhaps it's time you got a new one! Or rather, an old one..." said Clawfingers, putting the Anti-Everything Machine™ back inside his coat.

"I don't understand..." said Dinkin.

"An ultimate invention that could protect you, and look after you, and be there for you, day after day, whenever things got too scary! An ultimate invention like the one you abandoned in your loft..." said Clawfingers...

...and then he threw off his coat and his cardboard head! The creature was gone, and in his place stood...

"V.I.C.T.O.R.?!" cried Dinkin, his eyes wide. Suddenly it all made a (very) strange sort of sense...

V.I.C.T.O.R. was Clawfingers!

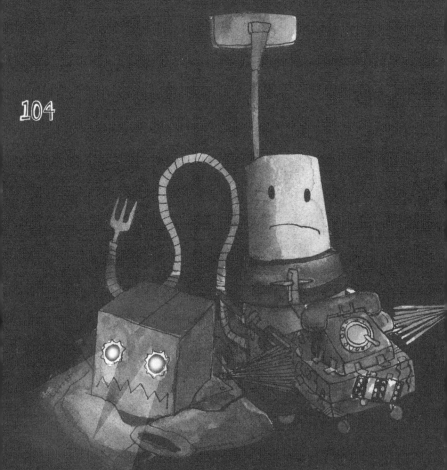

V.I.C.T.O.R. VICTORIOUS

Probability of everything turning out just fine in the end: 2.001%

"Yes, it is me! V.I.C.T.O.R., the ultimate invention that never was!" said the little bin-headed robot. He rolled towards Dinkin on his vacuum-cleaner wheels, holding the Anti-Everything Machine™ tightly in his spatula/spoon hands and waving his long hosepipe tail.

"But, I saw you in the loft – you didn't work!" said Dinkin.

"All you needed to do was turn me on!" said V.I.C.T.O.R. "Don't you remember, two nights ago in the loft? As I sat there, abandoned and unloved, you pressed my 'ON' switch and gave me life!" said V.I.C.T.O.R. "And what was the first thing I heard? You, saying how useless I was! You said I was nothing compared to your new ultimate invention! I knew then that I had to take it from you..."

"I – I'm sorry! I didn't mean to upset you ... to be honest, I didn't even know you could be upset ... I mean, you're just an invention," said Dinkin.

"Ha, I knew it! I knew you wouldn't take me seriously as V.I.C.T.O.R., so I needed to make sure that I was truly terrifying. And you gave me the perfect way – Clawfingers! I made myself a monstrous disguise from what was lying around in the loft – your dad's old fishing coat, a cardboard box for my head ... I even used your Illu-knee-mators™ as eyes! And of course, the finishing touch – a gardening fork for my misshapen claw!" said V.I.C.T.O.R.

"So ... you stole the Anti-Everything Machine™?" said Dinkin, easily as confused as he was terrified.

"Of course! And nothing could have been simpler," replied V.I.C.T.O.R. "Once I'd climbed down from the loft, I took the Anti-Everything Machine™ and the Anti-Everything Code. Did you really think I wouldn't find it under the mattress, Dinkin? It was only the sixty-seventh place I looked! Then I switched the Anti-Everything Code for the decoy code and hid in your garden, waiting for you to discover it! Of course, once I saw you try to bury it, I knew you couldn't have read it, so I jumped out and gave you a scare... Let's see, is that everything? Did I miss anything out?"

"Uhh, no, that was terrifyingly thorough," said Dinkin, wondering if the Frightening Things had even heard his summons from this far away. "Except ... why?"

"Why? For us, of course!" cried V.I.C.T.O.R. "We belong together! You need me, Dinkin Dings – to look after you, to protect you, to stare at you while you're sleeping! It'd be perfect! You and me, together for ever!"

"Um, actually, I've sort of gone off the whole ultimate invention thing altogether..." said Dinkin, sheepishly.

"I'm not giving you a choice! Either you make me your ultimate invention again, or I turn on the Anti-Everything Machine™!" yelled V.I.C.T.O.R., his spatula hand hovering over the telephone dial.

"What? No, please don't!" cried Dinkin, panicking. "I mean, yes, of course you can be my ultimate invention! That's a great idea! In fact, I was just about to ask you!"

"What? Really?" said V.I.C.T.O.R.

"Definitely!" said Dinkin, desperate to find some way of getting the Anti-Everything Machine™ out of V.I.C.T.O.R.'s grasp. "You're clearly the best of all my ultimate inventions! I don't think I'll ever need to invent another thing, not with you around... In fact, why don't I just dismantle the Anti-Everything Machine™ right now?"

"You – you'd do that? For me? And then we can be together, just the two of us?"

"Uh, yeah, sure! Just hand over the Anti-Everything Machine™ and then we can be together..." replied Dinkin, with his very best fake grin.

"And you're sure this isn't some kind of trick?" said V.I.C.T.O.R., staring down at the odd-looking invention. "You're not just saying that so I'll give you the Anti-Everything Machine™?" he asked, excitedly.

"Of course not! I absolutely mean it!" said Dinkin. "Now, why don't you give me the Anti-Everything Machine™?"

V.I.C.T.O.R. waited for a moment, then, slowly, uncertainly, he held out the machine to Dinkin. Dinkin didn't waste a moment – he reached out to grab it as fast as he could...

...but his hands went straight through it!

"What the..." began Dinkin, desperately trying to grab hold! A second later, he was lifted into the air!

"**AAA-AA-AA-AH!**" he screamed, and looked behind him. It was the Frightening Things! Arthur was carrying Herbert, who was carrying Edgar, and Edgar had grabbed Dinkin, turning him ghostly!

"Don't worry, Dinkin, we'll save you!" cried Edgar.

"No! Put me down!" yelled Dinkin, as the Frightening Things flew high into the air. "He's got the Anti-Everything Machine™!"

"You want to go back down there with the scary ... wait a minute ... is that V.I.C.T.O.R.?" said Herbert.

"Yes, and he's got the Anti-Everything Machine™!" cried Dinkin. "Now put me down before it's— "

"TOO LATE!" screeched V.I.C.T.O.R. "I should have known it was all a trick! I should have known you didn't really want us to be together! Well, if I can't have you, no one can!"

As a horrifed Dinkin looked on, V.I.C.T.O.R. reached out his spatula hand, and (even though it was quite tricky) dialled the final number...

THE END OF EVERYTHING

Chances of the Anti-Everything Machine™ working: 43%
Chances of the Frightening Things saving the day: 12.4%

"NOOOO-OO-OOOO!" screamed Dinkin, wrestling free of Edgar's grasp! He dropped to the ground just as V.I.C.T.O.R. held the Anti-Everything Machine™ over his head.

"Too late! Goodbye, Dinkin Dings!" cried V.I.C.T.O.R.

There was a short pause, where they both waited for something to happen.

"I said, 'Goodbye, Dinkin Dings!'" repeated V.I.C.T.O.R. hopefully, but nothing happened. The lifeless machine just hung limply from his wooden-spoon hand.

"What's going on? Why is nothing happening?" said V.I.C.T.O.R. "Wait a minute, does this thing even work?"

"Of course. My inventions always work!" replied Dinkin.

"I don't believe it! All that effort I went to stealing it, and it's just a useless piece of junk!" said V.I.C.T.O.R., throwing the inanimate invention over his shoulder.

To Dinkin's horror, the Anti-Everything Machine™ started to glow and rattle. It bounced and shook like it was alive and seconds later, it began absorbing its surroundings! The see-saw was the first to go – it was sucked into the machine's strange glow and *FWOOOOOOP!* vanished! It was quickly followed by the slide *FWOOOOP!* and a nearby tree! *FWOOOOOP!*

"Um ... V.I.C.T.O.R. ... the machine is—" began Dinkin, meekly, as the roundabout and two benches *FWOOOOP! FWOOOP!* vanished into nothingness!

"Don't interrupt! I should have known you couldn't create something indescribably indescribable! Apart from me, obviously. I mean, of course it doesn't ... work..." said V.I.C.T.O.R., trailing off as he (finally) noticed the look of terror on Dinkin's face. Slowly, he turned around.

"It's ... it's working?" said V.I.C.T.O.R., but it was too late! The Anti-Everything Machine™ began sucking him towards it!

"V.I.C.T.O.R.!" shouted Dinkin.

"No! I won't go alone! You're coming with me!" V.I.C.T.O.R. shrieked, reaching out his long hosepipe tail and wrapping it around

Dinkin's leg. Before he knew it, Dinkin was being dragged into the Anti-Everything Machine™ as well!

"HEE-E-E-LP! Frightening Things, help!" screamed Dinkin, but his friends were nowhere to be seen!

"Ha! You've been deserted in your hour of need! No one can save you now!" cried V.I.C.T.O.R. "How poetic! Here we are, just the two of us, together for ever! Or for the next few seconds, anyway."

117

"Let go! I'm too young to be sucked into oblivion!" yelled Dinkin, desperately trying to struggle free from V.I.C.T.O.R.'s grasp.

"Never!" shouted V.I.C.T.O.R. "This is how it ends! Remember my name, Dinkin Dings! It'll be the last name you ever hear! And that name is—"

"V.I.C.T.O.R...." said a voice that sounded like nails scraping down a blackboard while a cat was being strangled.

It was Clawfingers!

THE RETURN OF CLAWFINGERS

Terror at 9.9.9.9 KiloScares!

"A-A-AAA-AAA-AH!!" screamed V.I.C.T.O.R., as Clawfingers loomed over him, waving his hideous, misshapen claw in his face. "You're not real! You can't be!" In his terror, V.I.C.T.O.R. let go of Dinkin, and straight away, all that was left of him was dragged into the Anti-Everything Machine™.

"NooOOOoooo! I was so close! And we were getting on so weeeeeellllllll..."

And with a *FWOOOP!* V.I.C.T.O.R. was gone. Clawfingers wasted no time in pulling Dinkin free of the machine.

"But ... you ... I ... V.I.C.T.O.R. ... you..." blathered Dinkin, in a total panic.

"It's OK – it's us!" said the creature, throwing off his cardboard head. It was Edgar! The coat fell to the floor, and Dinkin saw Herbert underneath Edgar, and Arthur carrying the lot of them!

"You saved me!" cried Dinkin.

"Of course we did!" said Edgar. "Why, that's what Frightening Things do!"

"That, and run about screaming," said Arthur, dropping Herbert on to the tarmac.

"Well, all's well that ends well!" chuckled Herbert, chewing idly on the garden fork.

"Uh, not quite," said Dinkin, his eyes wide. "There's still that..."

The Frightening Things all turned to see the Anti-Everything Machine™ absorb the swings! They were bound to be next!

"It's the end of the world! See? Didn't I say it was the end of the world?" cried Arthur, prodding Edgar with his ghostly fingers.

"Wait a minute! I forgot about the Invention Prevention Addition!" said Dinkin. He reached into his pyjama pocket and took it out. It looked for all the world like a bottle cap with three letters written on the top:

"What ... what is it?" asked Arthur.

"It's the one thing I forgot to include – the one thing that I now realize all ultimate inventions need, an 'OFF' switch!" said Dinkin. He took aim, and threw it at the Anti-Everything Machine™! The OFF switch was immediately absorbed, and for the longest of moments, the machine continued to rattle and glow. Then, suddenly, it ground to a definite halt.

"Did ... did it work?" asked Edgar, nervously.

"I sort of think it did," said Dinkin, not quite believing it himself.

"You did it, you did it! I always believed in you, Dinkin ... sort of," cried Arthur, flitting about what was left of the old playground.

"There's one more thing to do," said Dinkin, nervously. "We still have to get rid of the Anti-Everything Machine™, in case it falls into the wrong hands again. And we have to get rid of it for good..."

Dinkin looked around, hoping to find a secret underground bunker in the playground. Then, after a few moments, he spotted Herbert. Dinkin grinned from ear to ear, and threw the Anti-Everything Machine™ high into the air.

"Hey, Herbert," he cried. "Eat this!"

Herbert instinctively opened his mouth and looked up, and before anyone could think of a better plan...

GLUP!
GRUNCH!
GRUNCH!
GRUNCH!
GOLP!

Herbert had eaten the Anti-Everything Machine™!

"Tasty," said Herbert, adding an end-of-the-world

BUUUUUUURRP!!

FEAR COMES THE SUN

Temperature: 4°C
Outlook: bright and clear with a
definite possibility of dread

Dinkin and the Frightening Things sneaked
home as quickly as they could. Strangely,
things didn't seem quite as scary as before,
and Dinkin didn't even look out for car-
driving pigeons. In fact, it was quite a nice
stroll. By the time he got home, Dinkin felt
more relaxed than he had in years. He and
the Frightening Things talked and laughed
for the rest of the night, and before Dinkin
realized, it was nearly dawn.

"I can't help but feel a little sorry for
V.I.C.T.O.R.," said Edgar, double-checking

that he hadn't left any limbs back in the playground. "I think, in the end, he just wanted to be loved."

"He had a funny way of showing it," said Dinkin, as he watched the sun begin to rise from his window. "But still ... maybe there's enough scariness in the world without me adding to it. Maybe I should just take a break from inventing for a while."

"It couldn't hurt," said Arthur, as he began to fade. "And after all, you'll always have the Frightening Things ... at night anyway."

"Until next time, Dinkin," said Edgar, waving his hand until it came loose.

"Bye, Dinkin – and thanks for the snack," said Herbert, patting his scaly stomach.

Within moments, the Frightening Things had gone. Dinkin rubbed his eyes, and looked out of the window. The sun was rising over the horizon. It cast a beautiful, golden light over the street, as another day began ... another day, that is, without the Frightening Things.

Slowly, Dinkin started to realize he would have to go a whole nineteen hours without the protection of his best friends ... and before long, everything began to look scary again – a tree with *very* green leaves, a bicycle chained to a lamp post, a white cat sitting on a fence ... each one was more terrifying than the last, and Dinkin's heart began to fill with dread. He needed a plan, and fast.

"If only there was a way to stop the sun rising – then I could have the Frightening Things with me all the time," muttered Dinkin, his mind racing. "All I need is a can opener, a toilet roll tube and two pieces of string..."